Warehouse 54

ALICE SAVAGE

Alice Savage grew up in a theatrical family and began writing plays in the fifth grade. As an English teacher of adult learners, she combines creative writing with a deep awareness of language to illuminate the worlds of immigrants and cultural explorers. She credits her multicultural family as inspiration. An author on many course books for Oxford University Press, Cambridge University Press, Pearson, and others, Alice has presented widely on the role of drama in language learning. She has published several award-winning one-act plays. Her dramatic fiction shows what happens when characters address challenges for which they may or may not be prepared. Alice lives in Houston.

First published by Gemma in 2025.

www.gemmamedia.org

Printed in the United States of America

978-1-956476-45-3

Library of Congress Cataloging-in-Publication Data

Names: Savage, Alice, 1962- author.
Title: Warehouse 54 / Alice Savage.
Other titles: Warehouse fifty four
Description: Boston : Gemma, 2025. | Series: Gemma open door |
Identifiers: LCCN 2024057321 (print) | LCCN 2024057322
(ebook) | ISBN 9781956476453 (trade paperback) |
ISBN 9781956476460 (epub)
Subjects: LCGFT: High interest-low vocabulary books. | Novels.
Classification: LCC PS3619.A8286 W37 2025 (print) |
LCC PS3619.A8286
(ebook) | DDC 813/.6--dc23/eng/20250122
LC record available at https://lccn.loc.gov/2024057321
LC ebook record available at https://lccn.loc.gov/2024057322

Cover by Laura Shaw Design

Named after the brightest star in the North-
ern Crown, Gemma is a nonprofit organiza-
tion that helps new readers acquire English
language literacy skills with relevant, engaging
books, eBooks, and audiobooks. Always orig-
inal, never adapted, these stories introduce
adults and young adults to the life-changing
power of reading.

Open Door

To Heiko, who sometimes works the
night shift

TABLE OF CONTENTS

1. Fall

Teddy and Kyle are walking home from the park. A cold wind is blowing. The two boys are hungry.

"Let's go to my house," says Teddy. "My mom made cookies."

Kyle likes cookies. He does not get them very often. "Sure," he says. "What kind?"

"Chocolate," says Teddy.

"My favorite!"

When they arrive, Teddy's mother, Dolores, is working in the yard. There are piles of bright yellow, orange, and red leaves. Dolores looks up when she sees the boys. She has big brown eyes like her son, Teddy. A green hat covers her long black hair.

"Don't go in the house, Teddy," Dolores says. "Your father is sleeping."

"But we want cookies," says Teddy. "We'll be quiet. I promise."

"Six-year-old boys can't be quiet. It's not possible," says Dolores. "I know you'll try, but your father needs to sleep."

Kyle looks confused.

"Teddy's dad isn't sick," Dolores says. "Paco sleeps in the day because he's working at night this week."

"He's a manager at a chemical plant," says Teddy.

"Does he make chemicals?" asks Kyle.

"Yes, big ones," says Teddy.

"The chemicals aren't big," says Dolores. "But the plant is, and it makes things *with* chemicals."

"What kinds of things?" asks Kyle.

"Big things," says Teddy.

"Do they explode?"

"No!" Dolores laughs. "He makes sure things *don't* explode!"

"Oh," says Kyle. He is disappointed.

"Paco's chemicals go into many things," says Dolores.

"He puts them on train cars," says Teddy.

"Trains? Train cars?" Kyle has more questions, but Dolores stops him.

"Look at you two! You're shaking from cold. Can you go over to Kyle's house?"

"I guess so," says Kyle. "But we don't have cookies."

"I'll bring cookies when I finish here," says Dolores.

Teddy looks at his mother. He wants to stay in his own house.

"That will be great, Miss Dolores," says Kyle. "Come on, Teddy. We can play with my trains."

Teddy follows Kyle down the street to a yellow house under a tall tree. He stops when he sees a lot of cars.

"I forgot to do something," says Teddy. "I need to go home."

"No, come!" Kyle pushes Teddy up the steps.

A dark-haired man in his twenties opens the door. He is Kyle's Syrian cousin, Rashid.

"Hi, Rashid," says Kyle.

"Kyle and Teddy!" says Rashid. "Come in." Suddenly, Teddy is inside the house.

Kyle's family is sitting around a fireplace. They are drinking tea in glasses. When the boys come in, they stop talking.

"I should go home," Teddy says.

"It's just relatives," says Rashid. "You know everyone here."

It is true. Teddy knows the family. They are nice, but Teddy feels nervous. He tries to step back, but the door is behind him. Then Lucky, Kyle's dog, jumps on Teddy. Teddy falls on Kyle's mother. Brita's tea spills.

"Don't worry, Teddy," says Brita. She gets up and cleans the tea.

Teddy looks at Kyle's Syrian family. They all have dark hair and brown eyes. Kyle's father Joe is sitting by the fire. Kyle's little brother, Ethan, is in his lap.

Rashid sits on the floor, and Rashid's mother, Mona, is in a chair by the window. Teddy tries to speak, but the words do not come.

Brita is the only non-Syrian in the room. Her blue eyes and red hair make her look different. Teddy nods, but he still does not speak.

"Would you like some fruit?" Brita holds out a plate of apples and oranges.

Kyle shakes his head. "We're not hungry."

"Then run upstairs," Brita says. "But take off your shoes."

The boys put their shoes in the pile by the door. Teddy follows his friend. He likes Kyle's room. It is long, and the bed is by a window. There is a train set on the floor. The boys make a small city with little houses and a hospital.

Suddenly, the wind blows harder. Teddy hears a loud noise, and a tree branch falls on the house. He remembers last summer. A storm blew down trees in their neighborhood. One of them fell on a neighbor's house. She almost died.

Kyle goes to the window and looks outside. "Your mother is coming!" he says. "Cookies!"

Teddy hears the door open. He hears his mother's voice, and he feels better. But the wind is still blowing, and he has a strange feeling. Something is going to happen. He does not know what, but he feels afraid.

2. *The Night Shift*

Back at Teddy's blue and white house, the wind blows the orange and red leaves against the windows. The sound wakes Paco. He looks at the time. It is 8 p.m. He can hear the storm, but not people. He checks his phone. There is a text from his wife. Dolores and Teddy are with the neighbors. They are staying for dinner.

That's good, Paco thinks. He likes Brita and her husband Joe and his family. Paco would like to join them, but he has to work. One time every year, his company shuts down the chemical plant. They empty the tanks and clean all the machines. They work all day and all night for one week.

Paco takes a shower and puts on his work clothes. He wears a blue uniform for protection from chemicals. He is cooking some eggs when Dolores comes in. Her hair is wet, and she is shaking from the cold.

"Oh, good! You're still here. I didn't want to miss you!" Dolores kisses her husband and sits at the kitchen table. "Teddy is going to sleep at Kyle's tonight."

"Oh, fun!"

Dolores sees the eggs. She gets up again. "Do you want me to do that for you?"

"It's fine. I'll do it." Paco heats up two tortillas.

"I'll make coffee then." Dolores gets up and goes to the coffee machine.

"It's OK, honey. There's coffee at work."

"I want to do something for you."

"You already do," Paco smiles. He puts the eggs and tortillas on a plate. "How was dinner?"

"Wonderful!" Dolores smiles. "Brita and Mona are funny. Brita starts to cook something. Then Mona takes over."

"Brita lets her sister-in-law cook?"

"Brita doesn't mind. And Mona likes it."

"Mona *is* a good cook," says Paco. "I like Syrian food."

"I guess that's why Brita doesn't mind," laughs Dolores. "Mona made rice with chicken. I didn't think Teddy would eat it, but he did."

"Good! Maybe he's getting more adventurous."

"I hope so." Dolores is not sure. "He didn't want to spend the night, at first."

"He's only six," says Paco.

"Yes, but he's very quiet, especially at Kyle's house. People make him nervous."

"Really? I never noticed," says Paco.

"He needs more confidence."

Paco thinks for a minute. "Maybe he can learn to ride a bike."

"That's a great idea!" Dolores gives Paco a cup of coffee. He drinks the hot black coffee and smiles.

"Bikes are fun!" Paco remembers his childhood. "My dad got me an old bike. It was too big for me, but he said I was growing, so I needed a big one. I fell off that bike so many times," Paco laughs. "But I learned."

"See! You got confidence," says Dolores.

"I used to carry my best friend in front. Sometimes there were three of us on one bike!" Paco says.

"Can you teach Teddy?" Dolores asks.

Paco's phone lights up, and he looks down. There is a text from his boss.

"What?" he says.

Dolores sits. "Can you teach Teddy to ride a bike?"

"Umm…sure," says Paco, looking up. "When I finish with the night shift, things will slow down. I'll do it then."

"Good. I want this maintenance to be over," says Dolores. "It's dangerous."

Paco stands up. "It'll be fine."

"Are you sure?"

"Yes. My job is to make sure everything is safe. There are some tanks I need to look at. Then I have reports to write."

Paco puts on heavy work boots. He takes his ID badge and opens the door. Cold air comes in.

"Paco," Dolores says. "Be careful!"

"I will. I promise," Paco turns and goes out into the rainy night. As he drives to work, Paco smiles. He remembers his childhood on Summer Street. It was fun to be a kid, to run around the neighborhood, climb trees, and go biking. He is looking forward to spending time with Teddy. He will teach his son all those things and more.

3. *Rashid's Story*

Teddy and Kyle are not sleepy. They are running up and down the stairs with Lucky. Lucky is not a big dog, but she makes a lot of noise. Joe and Brita are taking Mona home, so Rashid goes upstairs.

When Teddy sees Rashid, he stops running and sits by the window. Kyle looks at his cousin.

"Do you want to hear a story?" Rashid asks. Kyle goes to get his books, but Rashid shakes his head. "I'm going to turn off the light. You guys get in bed. I'll make up a story."

Rashid sits in a big chair. Teddy and Kyle make a bed on the floor. Then they lie down with Lucky. Rashid turns off the light, but there is a small night-light on the wall. It looks like a camel. Rashid looks at the camel. Then he looks at the carpet on the floor. Finally, he begins his story.

"In the mountains of Syria, there was a small city. In the city, there was an important house. The house was four stories high. It had a flower garden. The windows had blue, red, and yellow glass. The colored light made the house feel special, especially in the afternoon."

"Was it your house?" asks Kyle.

"No, this was a thousand years ago," says Rashid. "A rich trader lived there with his family. He bought and sold beautiful things."

"Like what?" asks Kyle.

"Carpets, like the one right here in your bedroom."

Rashid points to the red and black carpet on Kyle's floor.

"He also brought tea, spices, and other wonderful things. When he came home, he gave presents to his family. He told stories about his adventures. They liked hearing about the camels that traveled over the mountains. But they liked hearing about the ocean best. None of them had seen the ocean before.

"'The water changes colors,' said the father. 'It can look blue, green, silver, or black, but it's never only one color. And it has feelings. Sometimes it is peaceful, and sometimes it is angry. Sometimes the wind doesn't blow, and the boats don't move. It's not easy to cross the ocean on a boat,' said the father.

"The family liked his stories and the gifts," Rashid continues, "but as you know, something always happens in a story. One day, the father came home with only one carpet. He did not show it to anyone. He took the carpet to a room at the top of the house. Then he closed the door. 'No one can go in there,' he said. 'Not even you!' he told his wife. 'Or you,' he said to his children.

"Their father's words made the children curious. They wanted to see the carpet, but they were afraid of their father. Then one day, a boy named Abdul couldn't wait. Abdul went to the fourth floor. He opened a blue window and climbed outside. Carefully, he went around the outside of the building. Then he came in through a red and gold window. There he found the special carpet.

"At dinner that night, Abdul did not appear. His mother called his name. The other children looked for him. No one found him. When his father heard the news, he went upstairs and opened the door."

"Was Abdul there?" asks Kyle.

"No, Abdul wasn't there. The carpet wasn't there. And the window was open."

"It was a flying carpet!" says Kyle.

"Yes, it was," says Rashid. "Abdul was flying over the ocean. He only had to think about the ocean, and the carpet took him there. At first, Abdul was afraid, but he was excited, too. When he finally looked down, he saw the big black ocean under the night sky. It wasn't only black, though. It was just as his father had said. There was silver moonlight on the waves. The boats had yellow lights. Abdul also saw the mountains of his own country. Above the mountains, there were stars."

"What did he do next?" asks Kyle.

"Well, Abdul thought it was beautiful. Then he had another thought. He wanted to show it to his family. The carpet followed his thought. It took him back to his house. He went in through the red window on the fourth floor. His father was waiting for him there."

"Was his father angry?"

"No."

"Why not?"

"His father was proud of him."

"That's strange," says Kyle.

"Why do you say that?" Rashid asks.

"Abdul broke the rules," Kyle says, "and he didn't get in trouble."

"I know. It was a test."

"What kind of test?"

"Maybe the father wanted to take a child with him on his travels. Which child would he take?"

"Abdul?" Kyle looks thoughtful.

"Exactly. Because Abdul was brave and curious. And he cared about his family."

"I'm curious," says Kyle.

"Yes, you are, and sometimes you don't follow the rules. Maybe you'll take over your father's business," Rashid laughs. "Anyway, it was just a story. Now lie down next to Teddy. I'll stay here until you sleep."

Kyle falls asleep quickly, but Teddy cannot sleep. When he closes his eyes, he thinks about being alone over the dark ocean. He hears the wind blowing. He is scared.

"I want to go home," he says.

"Are you sure?"

"Yes, I want my mom," Teddy says.

A few minutes later, Dolores is at the door. She thanks Rashid and takes Teddy's hand. They walk home through the rain. A few minutes later, Teddy falls asleep in his own bed with his mother next to him.

4. Rules

Paco arrives at the chemical plant. He shows his ID at the front entrance. Then he parks and looks up. The place is like a small city, but it is a city of pipes and tanks. The pipes are many sizes. They carry different chemicals. He knows each one and its purpose. Some of the chemicals are dangerous, so Paco checks the tanks and pipes often.

Today, workers are cleaning the tanks and fixing pipes. Paco asks them about their families. Then he asks about the equipment. "Is anything unusual?"

"Nothing to report," says one man.

"All under control," says another.

"Everything is right on schedule," says a woman. Her name is Bunny. She is taller than Paco, and she has a loud voice.

Paco asks Bunny to stand outside the tanks so he can go inside and check for problems. There are rules. People have to work in pairs. No one can go in the tank unless someone is watching. It might be dangerous.

Paco puts on a mask. Then he climbs inside the first tank. The air is still. Paco walks around and looks at the walls. He takes photos. Then Paco checks the other tanks.

The last one is Tank 8. It looks different. There are cracks in the walls. Paco stays in the tank for a long time. He makes notes. It is hard to breathe, so he works quickly. He takes some photos. Then he goes back outside. He looks around. Bunny is gone.

Paco sighs. He goes to the control room. It is warm inside, and his glasses fog up. He cleans them. Then he writes up the safety violations. When he finishes, Paco sits back and looks at the computer screens. He can see workers in blue. Then he sees Bunny. Now she is driving a forklift. She is not wearing her hard hat or safety glasses.

Paco sighs. Bunny is a good worker, but she does not like to follow rules. Paco makes a note. Then he looks again. Now the forklift is empty, and a man is talking to Bunny. He looks away from the camera with his glasses in his hand. Bunny says something, and they laugh. The man puts his hand on Bunny's shoulder. She smiles. Then she points at the camera. Paco feels like she is pointing at him.

The man steps back. They both put on their glasses. Paco is relieved. *Bunny knows I'm watching*, he thinks. Then the man turns around. Paco is surprised to see Karl. Karl is Paco's boss. He will be harder to control, but Paco must do his job. He makes another note.

5. Pick Up

The next week, Dolores texts Kyle's mother from her car. *Hi Brita, I've got an appointment. Can you pick up Teddy when you get Kyle from school?*

Brita texts Dolores: *I'm still at work. Is it OK if Kyle's cousin Rashid goes? He's home today.*

Dolores texts Brita: *Oh, the happiness of a big family. Is it OK with Rashid?*

Brita texts Dolores: *Of course. He's getting Kyle anyway.*

Next, Brita texts Rashid: *Can you get Teddy, too?*

Rashid does not text back. Rashid's phone is on his bike. He is sitting by a river with his girlfriend, Olivia.

"Tell me about Aleppo," she says. "I've been looking at pictures of Syria. I can't believe your city is eight thousand years old."

"It's true," says Rashid. "Aleppo is on the old trading roads between China and Europe. Spices, carpets, and cloth from all over the world came through there."

"That's so cool!" says Olivia. "I'd love to see it."

"When I was growing up, we lived near a place for traders. They slept next to their camels in special doorways."

"Wow, so much history," says Olivia. "I would love to see that."

"I would love to show you!" says Rashid. He looks sad for a moment. "I'm not sure it's still there." Then he smiles. "We need a time machine. We could go back ten years and have a great visit."

"I want to go back 1,000 years and see the camels," says Olivia.

"Really?" Rashid laughs. "You don't have to go that far back."

"Any time is OK. I just want to sit in a café and watch people."

"Funny, I like getting coffee from a drive-through. It's so much faster."

"Is faster better?" asks Olivia. "In a car, you separate from people. In the streets, you connect."

Rashid looks at Olivia. "You really should travel," he says. "You see things that other people don't."

"Do I?" She looks up at him. "That's a nice thing to say."

"I like that about you," says Rashid.

Their eyes meet. Rashid kisses Olivia. She puts her arm around him. The phone lights up and buzzes. But they do not see it or hear it.

Back at her school, Brita looks at her phone. No message. She picks up her papers and goes to the car. First, she picks up Ethan at his babysitter. Then she drives to Kyle and Teddy's school. No one is there. *Maybe Rashid got the message*, she thinks. But when Brita and Ethan arrive, the house is empty.

Brita lets Ethan watch TV. She calls the school. No one answers. She looks out the window. There is a ball and some yellow and red leaves, but no boys.

Then Brita sees Rashid and Olivia on their bikes. Brita's heart jumps. She goes outside just as Olivia is leaving.

Rashid looks up and suddenly remembers. "I was supposed to pick up Kyle," he says.

"And Teddy. Didn't you get my text?"

"I'm sorry. I forgot." Rashid feels terrible.

"We can talk about that later. We need to find the boys."

"I'm on it," Rashid gets back on his bike.

"Look at your phone!" Brita calls after him. "Call me if you find them!"

Brita goes inside and picks up Ethan. He does not want to leave the TV, but Brita cannot leave him alone.

She carries him to Teddy's house. Paco's truck is there, but Paco is probably asleep. She will have to wake him.

Just then, Dolores's car arrives. Dolores gets out and sees Brita's face. "What happened?"

"Rashid forgot to pick up the boys. They're not at school!"

"OK," Dolores says. "Let's not panic." She opens the front door. Then she stops. Paco is on the floor. He is not moving. Dolores runs and almost falls over a train. "Paco! Are you OK?"

Paco turns over and opens his eyes. "I'm fine, why?"

Dolores stops. "Then why are you on the floor?"

"I'm playing with trains," he says. "I just fell asleep for a minute."

"Paco, are you . . ." Dolores stops when she hears voices. Teddy and Kyle come in with boxes of trains.

"Hi, mom," they both say. The mothers run to the boys. They hug each boy.

"We were so scared!" says Brita. "Where were you?"

"Rashid forgot to get the boys from school," says Paco.

"I know!" say Brita and Dolores at the same time.

"But we didn't know you had them!" says Brita.

"Teddy asked his teacher to call me. I guess your phone was off."

"I was driving," says Dolores.

Dolores looks at Paco. "Can you text us next time?"

"I will. I promise," says Paco. "I'm sorry. I'm not thinking clearly this week."

"Dad," says Teddy, "We need your help. We want to make a chemical plant for the trains."

Paco turns to the boys. "What if we use those boxes to build it here?"

Dolores sighs. Then she turns to Brita. "I need a cup of tea. You?" She goes to the kitchen, and Brita follows.

"I'm sorry about Rashid," says Brita. "I know he wants to help, but he doesn't always think."

"I know. And I probably worry too much about Teddy. When he came home the other night, he was a little upset."

"Is he OK?" asks Brita. "So sorry about that. I think Rashid was telling them a story. His stories can be a little strange."

"Teddy gets scared easily. But I need to remember this. Teddy solved the problem. He called Paco, and they made it home safely."

"Right," says Brita. "And listen. He's OK now."

They hear laughter in the living room.

"It seems like there are three boys in there," says Dolores.

"Paco is a great dad," says Brita.

"He is," says Dolores. "He makes me a little crazy sometimes, but I don't know what I would do without him!"

6. Mr. Careful

Back at work, Paco goes to a safety meeting. First, he talks about the older machines. Some of the pipes are getting old. He worries about Tank 8. He has questions about the warehouses. If the chemicals get wet, they might leak out. Then they are dangerous.

"They could explode," Paco says.

"I know, Mr. Careful," says Karl, "but a lot of things have to go wrong before that happens."

Bunny often calls Paco "Mr. Careful." This is the first time Paco's boss says it.

"I have some ideas," says Paco.

"Put them in your report. I'll look at it later," says Karl.

At that moment, Bunny walks in. She gets a cup of coffee and sits next to Karl.

"Sorry I'm late," she says. "I was checking the warehouse."

Karl turns to Bunny, "Everything OK?"

"Yeah, no problem. They're bringing in the new chemicals today."

"Who is?" asks Paco.

"Some guys." Bunny crosses her arms.

"Are they trained?"

Bunny shrugs. "Sure. Forklift training. They know how to move chemicals, Paco. Don't worry about it."

Paco shakes his head. "I know, but—"

"We need to think about the start-up," Bunny interrupts.

"I'm thinking about our arms and legs," says Paco.

Bunny rolls her eyes and looks at Karl. "Nothing is going to happen in the warehouse."

"And breathing," says Paco. "I like breathing, too."

"Breathing is good," says Karl. "And we *are* thinking about safety, Paco. In fact, I have good news. You are getting an alarm system. The guys are putting it in tomorrow. They'll be all over the plant, even in the warehouses."

"Great!" says Paco. "That will tell us *after* an accident happens. Now if we can just stop the accident *before* it happens."

Karl closes his laptop. "I hear you, Paco, but I agree with Bunny. We need to focus on the start-up. Now, is there anything else?"

Paco moves uncomfortably.

"There is one more thing. Some of the workers aren't wearing protection. There are reports of people taking off their masks and not wearing safety glasses."

"*Your* reports," says Bunny.

"Not *only* mine," says Paco.

Karl sighs. "I understand, Paco. But you know it gets hot in there, and sometimes people need to talk. It's hard to talk with a mask on."

Paco does not answer. He just looks at Karl, and Karl finally opens his laptop again. "OK, Paco. We'll send out an email. Everyone needs to wear protection."

Bunny looks at Paco, "Happy now?"

"Yes," says Paco. "I'm happy when people go home to their families and not to the hospital."

When the meeting is finally over, Paco goes outside. It feels good to breathe the cold air. He looks out over the parking lot and sees the first morning light. The clouds are breaking up, and the sunlight turns them pink and gold.

7. *The Donut Shop*

Paco goes to his truck. He is too tired to drive, and it is not safe. He sleeps for ten minutes. Then he goes home. When he walks in the door, Dolores and Teddy are at the table.

"Hi, honey," says Dolores.

Paco kisses her and hugs Teddy. Then he sits down and takes off his boots. "It's good to be home."

"Coffee?" Dolores gets up.

"I think I've had enough. I'll just sit here for a while."

"Was it a hard night?" Dolores asks.

"A difficult meeting. I'll tell you about it later."

Teddy looks at his father. "Dad?"

"Yes, Teddy?"

"Can you drive me to school?"

"Son, I would love to, but I'm too . . ." Paco stops when he sees Teddy's sad face. "Sure."

Dolores shakes her head. "Your dad needs to rest."

"It's OK," says Paco. "A few more minutes won't matter." He goes to the bathroom and puts cold water on his face. He can hear Dolores talking to Teddy.

"Brita will pick you up after school," she says. "You can go to Kyle's."

"Do I have to?"

"Yes, for a little while."

Paco comes back. "Ready, Teddy?" he asks.

"Ready, dad!" says Teddy. Father and son get in the truck.

"Don't you want to go to Kyle's?" Paco asks.

"I like home better."

"But you can't stay home all the time," says Paco.

"Why not?"

"It's part of growing up. You need to have adventures."

"I'm not really into adventures," says Teddy.

"Why do you say that?"

"I like to be at home," says Teddy. "Is that bad?"

Paco looks at Teddy. Then he passes the school and drives to a donut shop.

"What are you doing, dad?"

"Having an adventure."

"But I'll be late to school!"

"Well, sometimes when you are having an adventure, it's OK to be a little late."

"I'll get in trouble!"

"No, you won't. *I* might get in trouble, but *you* won't," Paco laughs. "It's OK. I'm used to it."

They get out of the truck and go inside the warm shop. The donuts smell delicious. Paco gives some money to Teddy.

"What is this for?" Teddy says.

"So you can buy a donut."

"Can't you buy it for me?"

"I don't know what kind you like."

"Yes, you do! Chocolate."

"Oh right, but I need to check my phone. You buy them. Tell the woman you want two chocolate donuts."

"Two?"

"One for me," says Paco.

Teddy goes to the woman. She is busy, and she does not see him. He waits quietly. Then he looks at his dad. Paco smiles and nods. "I'm going to that table over there." Paco leaves Teddy.

A few minutes later, Teddy comes to the table. He is smiling and carrying a small white bag. He takes out two donuts and gives one to his father.

"Your mother and I have been talking," says Paco before taking a bite. "We're going to get you a bike."

Teddy eats more slowly. There is chocolate on his face. "Why? I can't ride a bike."

"I'll teach you Sunday after church."

"I don't know if I *want* to ride a bike," says Teddy putting down his donut.

"No, you don't know. That's why I'm going to show you. Don't decide before you try it."

"OK," says Teddy.

"Maybe you'll like it. If you do, we'll ride to the river."

"OK," says Teddy.

Back in the truck, Paco cleans the chocolate from Teddy's face. "Your mom says you are nervous around new people, but I will tell you a secret."

"What's that?"

"Everybody is."

"No, they aren't. Rashid's not nervous. He's always talking."

"Well, that's true," Paco says. "Rashid has a lot of confidence, but some people talk when they are nervous."

"Is Rashid nervous?"

"Maybe. I get nervous with strangers, too."

"No, you don't."

"Yes, I do. Your mother does, too."

"No, she doesn't."

"She does. We're just brave. To be brave you have to do scary things. Sometimes you have to talk to strangers. Sometimes you have to disagree with people. I do it all the time. And do you know what?"

"What?"

"It gets easier."

"How do you know?"

"Because you just bought your own donut! You were scared, and you did it anyway."

"Oh," says Teddy.

"Nothing terrible happened. And it was a really good donut."

"It was," says Teddy.

8. Busy

Saturday comes. Dolores and Teddy are putting more leaves in bags. Rashid and Kyle walk by with Lucky.

"We're going to the dog park," says Kyle. "Want to come?"

Teddy turns and looks at his mother. "Can you come with us?"

"No, I'll just finish up here. You go," says Dolores. "I have to check on your father. He's still sleeping."

She watches Teddy and his friend walk away. At the corner, Teddy turns and waves. Dolores waves back. Then she looks at the fallen leaves. There is still work to do, but she feels tired. Dolores finishes one more bag and goes inside. Paco is awake.

"Do you want coffee?" he asks.

"Sure," says Dolores, but when he hands her a cup, she puts it down. "I'm so glad you are done with that maintenance," she says. "We can have our life back."

"I know," Paco says. Then he looks around. "Don't we have cookies?"

Dolores points to a plate on the table.

Paco laughs. "I think I am losing my mind." He takes one. "Where's Teddy?"

"He went to the dog park with Rashid and Kyle."

Paco nods. "That's good. I like that family."

"We should have them for dinner," says Dolores.

"Yes," says Paco. "Now that I'm off the night shift, we can, and maybe I can fix the fence."

"And teach Teddy to ride a bike."

"And help Miss Polly rebuild her house."

"And plan a trip to Mexico. My mother really wants us to visit."

"And paint the bathroom."

They look at each other and laugh. Then Paco's phone lights up.

"Ugh," says Dolores. "It's work, isn't it?"

"Yep." Paco reads the message. "Bunny's mother is sick, so she's taking some time off."

"What does that mean?" Dolores gets up and pours her coffee out.

"I'll just have to do a few extra things. Nothing to worry about."

"You have to do her work now?" Dolores turns on the water.

"It's her mother, Dolores. I have to help."

Dolores nods. "I understand. I just hope it's not too much."

"She's responsible for the warehouse," says Paco finishing his coffee. "I'll just have to move the chemicals from the warehouse to the tanks. It'll be fine."

9. Dinner

A few days later, Dolores comes home with shopping bags. She has chicken, red sauce, rice, and cheese. She is cooking Mexican food for Brita and Joe. Dolores calls her mother in Mexico for help. They talk for a long time. Then Dolores's mother asks about Teddy.

"I want to see him," she says.

"And you will. We'll visit next summer," says Dolores. She puts the phone on speaker and looks for tortillas while she talks.

"Don't wait so long!" her mother says. "Your father and I are getting old."

"You are not old," says Dolores, still looking for the tortillas. "Listen, I have to go, mom. I'll call you later."

"All right," says her mother. "But tell your husband to take a break. He works too much. You need to come to Mexico."

"I promise," says Dolores. "Next summer."

"I want to see you. I need to make sure you're OK."

"I'm fine! Why wouldn't I be?"

"I don't know. Are you happy?"

"Yes! I'll be happier when I find the tortillas."

"I hate to think of you all alone."

"I'm not alone. Paco is here," says Dolores. "Now, I have to go."

Finally, Dolores hangs up. She needs some fresh air, so she walks to the store. Her mother is a good person, but she thinks Dolores made a mistake when she married Paco.

On the way back, Dolores stops to watch the boys. They are running and laughing in the leaves. The sky is blue, and the sunlight looks gold. *I love my life*, she thinks.

Dolores takes the tortillas inside. She puts chicken inside each tortilla. Then she covers them with red sauce and adds cheese. They are ready to cook. Dolores sets the table. She turns on the oven and puts in the food. Then she looks out the window. It is six o'clock. *Where is Paco?* Dolores does not try to call or text him. He cannot take his phone into the plant.

Teddy comes inside. "I fell and hurt my leg," he says.

Dolores takes Teddy to the bathroom. She cleans the injury and covers it. "Does it hurt?" she asks.

"Yes, but I didn't cry," says Teddy, "even when I saw the blood."

"You are brave, Teddy!"

Teddy smiles. "Where's dad? I want to show him."

"He'll be here soon. Did Kyle go home?" Dolores hears her phone ring, but she lets it go to messages.

"Yes, he's coming back for dinner."

When Teddy is cleaned up, Dolores goes back to the kitchen. She hopes Paco is in his car. He usually texts or calls when he is on his way home. Paco's message comes from the company phone: *I have to pick up some chemicals from the warehouse. Then I'll leave. I promise.*

There is a noise at the door. When Dolores opens it, Brita is holding a covered plate and Joe has drinks. Kyle has a box of trains.

"I made a cake," says Brita.

Dolores smiles. "Wonderful! I made a tres leches cake. We'll have two desserts!"

"I can eat two desserts," says Brita.

"So can I," says Dolores.

"Where's Paco?" says Joe.

"He's at work. He should be here, soon." Dolores stands back to let them in.

"It smells good!" says Brita.

"Do you like red enchiladas?" asks Dolores.

"I love them!" says Brita. "I love anything when someone else cooks it!"

Dolores laughs and invites them to sit down. She is serving drinks when her phone rings again. "That must be

Paco," she says, but when she sees the number, she frowns.

"What is it?" asks Bunny.

"It's his boss," says Dolores. She waits for a moment. Then she answers. "Hello, Karl?"

"Dolores?" says Karl.

"Yes, Karl, what is it?"

"Is Paco there?"

"Not yet. Do you want him to call you?"

"Yes."

"Is something wrong?" Dolores stands up. Her voice gets louder.

"There's a fire at the plant," says Karl. "We want to find everyone, and Paco isn't answering. I'm sorry to be calling, but I thought maybe he was home."

Dolores feels cold. She uses an app to find Paco's phone. "His phone is still in his truck. It's in the parking lot."

"That means he's still at work," says Karl.

Now Dolores feels panic. "Where is the fire?"

"It's in a building where we keep chemicals. It's usually empty, so I'm not too worried. But we need to check."

Dolores takes a quick breath. "Paco was getting chemicals from the warehouse."

There is silence on the other side. Then Karl says, "Right. Listen. We'll find him. I'll tell him to call you."

"Please do!" she says. "Right away." Then she puts down the phone and looks at Brita and Joe. "It seems Paco has gotten lost in the plant some-where," she laughs and stands up. "I'm just going to check dinner." Dolores quickly leaves and goes into the kitchen. She leans against the doorway. She is breathing hard. Her hands are shaking. Then the phone rings again.

10. *The Warehouse*

It is almost dark when Paco arrives at the warehouse. This part of the plant is empty. There are old tanks. The company uses newer tanks now, but the old ones are still in the back. Trees grow around them. Plastic bags blow in the wind. They catch on trees and pipes.

Paco drives the company truck slowly along the front of the building. He is looking for Building 54. When he finds it, the big door is open. He can see bags of chemicals inside. He sees water on the floor inside.

Paco is angry. When the doors are open, rain can get in. Water can make the chemicals dangerous. Bunny knows that. He will have to report another safety violation.

Paco goes inside and turns on the light. It is suddenly too bright. Paco has to close his eyes. When he opens them, he sees more boxes and bags of chemicals. Many of the bags are taller than he is. Paco finds the chemicals he needs. Then he looks for the forklift. The workers left it by a far wall.

Paco feels a little sick. *I really need to sleep*, he thinks. Paco goes over to the forklift and puts on his hard hat and glasses. Then he climbs inside and turns it on. The machine starts, but a spark hits the floor. Paco turns. He sees orange, then red, then black smoke. Paco jumps out of the forklift. One of the bags is on fire. He looks for something to put the fire out, but the safety box is not there. The workers took it off the wall when they put in the alarm.

The alarm goes off.

The fire gets bigger.

The fire can't reach the forklift, Paco thinks. Paco starts to get back in. Then he sees another open bag of chemicals. He tries to pull it toward him, but it is wet and heavy. The fire is close to the forklift now, and it is bigger. The hot air smells like chemicals.

Paco gives up on the forklift. The chemicals are burning. He must save himself now. He turns to run. He falls over a pipe. His hard hat falls off. Then he feels a hot wind in his hair. It sounds like an oven turning on, but louder. Paco gets up and runs.

There is an explosion, and the wind lifts him into the air. Paco puts his hands in front of him. When he hits the floor, his right hand makes a cracking sound. It is broken, but he does not feel pain. *If I only break my hand, I will be lucky*, he thinks. He uses his other hand to push himself up. He is still inside the building, but the door is closer.

Paco tries to breathe, but there is no air. A red light flashes, and he can hear the alarm. He climbs toward the black square of night. The opening is close now, but he is moving slowly.

Suddenly, there is a second explosion. Parts of the forklift fly through the air. Paco's body rises again, and the wind pushes him into the darkness.

Then he is on the ground, and something hits him hard. He cannot move. Right before he passes out, he realizes he is alone. All his plans for this night have changed. He is not going to eat Mexican food or laugh with his family and friends. Instead, he is alone under the night sky.

"I'm sorry, Dolores," Paco says. Then he closes his eyes.

The alarm stops. Now there is only the sound of the fire.

11. The Hospital

The boys are in Teddy's bedroom when Teddy hears his mother's cry. Teddy knows it is about his father. He puts down his truck. He covers his ears. He cannot stop the sound. Even Kyle looks scared.

A few minutes later, Dolores comes in. Her eyes are red. She hugs Teddy and kisses his hair. "There's been an accident at the plant," she says. "Your father is missing."

"I know," says Teddy. "Can we go there and find him?"

"No, we have to wait." Dolores holds Teddy's hand. "Your father is careful, and he does everything right. He's going to be OK."

"He's not always careful," says Teddy. "Sometimes he breaks the rules."

"What do you mean?"

"We got donuts last week."

"Oh, Teddy!" says Dolores. "Donuts aren't dangerous."

"I know, but he broke the rules. I was late for school."

"There's a difference. Your father wanted to spend time with you. It wasn't about safety."

Teddy thinks for a minute. "I'm glad he did, then."

"Me, too." Dolores hugs Teddy.

Brita opens the door, "Dolores, I hate to bother you, but something is burning."

"Yes, there's a fire at the chemical plant," says Dolores.

"No, here! Something's burning here!"

Suddenly, the house's smoke alarm goes off. Dolores runs to the kitchen. Smoke is coming out of the oven and filling the room. She turns it off. Joe opens windows. Cold air blows in, and the alarm stops.

Brita sees Dolores's panic. She tells Joe to take Kyle home. When the smoke is gone, she closes the windows.

"I'm so sorry Dolores," Brita says when she hears the news. "Paco is all about safety. He'll be OK."

"I keep telling myself that." Dolores's brown eyes fill with tears.

"He will."

"But you don't know that," says Teddy. "No one knows."

Brita doesn't have an answer, so she makes tea. Dolores and Teddy come to the table, but no one drinks.

Finally, Karl calls. "We found Paco," he says.

Dolores takes a deep breath, "Is he alive?"

"Yes, but he's injured. He got out of the building, but a part of the wall hit him. He's on his way to the hospital now."

Dolores does not stop. She just goes to the car. Brita and Teddy follow her.

"Let me drive," Brita says.

Dolores gives Brita the keys. At the hospital, Brita drops Dolores in front. She watches her friend walk through the glass doors. Dolores is not wearing any shoes. Brita parks the car and takes Teddy inside. Dolores is standing under bright, hospital lights. "The doctors say he is badly hurt," she says.

"Is he awake?" Brita asks.

"No, he's not. I asked if he'll live through the night."

"What did they say?"

"They don't know."

12. Waiting

Dolores and Teddy wait. The doctors say Paco has a broken hand and a head injury. They are giving him blood. Then they tell Dolores more bad news. Paco will lose his leg.

Dolores takes a deep breath. "But will he live?"

"It's hard to say," says one doctor. "We are watching him carefully, but we can't promise."

The next day, Brita brings shoes for Dolores, and clean clothes, toys, and a book for Teddy. Mother and son stay in the waiting room. They do not go home to shower. They do not go to church on Sunday.

On Sunday night, there is still no change. Dolores wants Teddy to go to school, so Brita brings him to the yellow house. When Brita gives him food, he eats. When his teachers ask questions, he answers. After school, he sits next to the window and looks outside. There are always people around, but he feels alone.

Sometimes they talk about his father.

"Isn't he a safety specialist?" asks Rashid's mother one day. Mona is visiting. She likes to cook for the family.

"Yes," says Brita. "He is good at his job, too. But he was in the wrong place at the wrong time."

"How did the fire start, anyway?" Rashid looks up from his computer.

"His boss says workers left the door open, and water got in. Do you remember that storm last week? They think rain mixed with chemicals inside. They leaked out of the bags. Then a spark from the forklift started the fire."

"Why did they leave the door open?" Rashid asks.

"Not all the workers had keys, so when they were bringing in the chemicals for the start-up, they left the door open for each other."

"Why didn't they ask for keys?" Mona adds spices to the stew.

"I don't know," says Brita. "They didn't know this was going to happen." She puts rice and vegetables on the table.

"I would have asked for keys," says Rashid.

"Maybe they didn't want to," says Joe.

"Why not?" Brita looks at her husband,

"Could be different reasons," Joe says. "Maybe they wanted to finish quickly. Or they didn't think safety was important. Or maybe they were afraid to ask."

"Why would they be afraid to ask?" Mona frowns. "That doesn't make sense."

"Sometimes my workers don't like to ask me for things," says Joe.

"Why? You're not scary," Brita looks at him with curiosity.

Joe nods. "That's your opinion. I think I'm nice, too, but that doesn't matter. It's about how *they* feel."

"I guess," says Mona.

"Sometimes people are the problem, not the equipment. All these things are important when you work in a chemical plant." Joe sits at the table.

"And I'm happy you don't. . ." Brita starts to say. Then she notices Teddy and stops herself. "Come eat," she tells him. Brita puts rice on Teddy's plate. "Your father is a strong man," she tells him. "He worked hard to make that plant safe."

"Yeah, but it wasn't enough," says Teddy quietly. "My dad might die because those people didn't care."

Everyone looks at Teddy. Teddy looks at the yellow rice and green vegetables.

"I feel sick," he says.

13. Awake

A few days later, Brita and Teddy go to the empty house for clothes. More leaves are in the yard. Inside, it looks like people left quickly. There are glasses in the living room. The plates are still on the table, and it smells like smoke.

Brita washes and puts away the dishes. She goes through the food and makes two piles. One pile is good food. She puts that away. She throws away the bad food. The kitchen is empty now, and it feels sad without Dolores.

Back at the yellow house, Brita puts Ethan to bed. Teddy asks to go to the hospital, so Rashid drives him. When they arrive, Dolores is with the doctors.

Rashid sits with Teddy in a small waiting room. The door says "ICU."

"This is the place where doctors save lives," says Rashid. "It's very exciting."

"I don't think it's exciting," says Teddy.

Rashid stops. "OK. What do you think is exciting?"

"Exciting is riding a bike and jumping in the leaves. This isn't exciting. It's just sad."

"Sorry," says Rashid. "I was thinking like a doctor. I guess it's exciting for doctors, but it's different for families."

"Yes," says Teddy. "I'm not excited."

"But think about this," says Rashid. "Your dad might live because of doctors."

"I don't want to think about that. I'm angry."

"I'm trying to give you hope," says Rashid.

"My dad promised to teach me to ride a bike."

"He did?"

"Yes, but he can't. He's never going to ride a bike."

"He might."

"With one leg?" Teddy shakes his head.

"Well, maybe he can get another one."

"Another leg?"

"Yes, there are all kinds of legs now. People can walk and run and even go upstairs. Did you know there are legs that you can move by thinking?"

"Thinking? Like how you move a real leg?"

"Yes," says Rashid.

"But it's not your real leg?"

"No, it's a bionic leg."

Rashid takes out his phone. He shows Teddy videos of people with artificial legs. One shows a woman riding a bike. Another shows a man dancing.

Teddy suddenly laughs. "If you can move your leg with thoughts, could anyone do it?"

"Why not?"

"What if I use my thoughts to control my dad's leg? Like maybe he wants to go to the kitchen, but I want him to stay in the living room. I can use my thoughts to stop his leg." Teddy starts laughing. "That would be funny."

Rashid thinks about Paco with legs going in different directions. He starts laughing, too. "You can make him climb on the table!"

Teddy does not want to laugh at his dad, but he cannot help it. "I can make him dance on the table!" he says, and they laugh harder. Laughing stops the sadness and anger. Something changes inside Teddy.

Dolores comes out and sees them. At first, she thinks Teddy is crying. Then she sees he is laughing.

"What's so funny?" she asks.

Teddy tries to explain. "Dad with a bionic leg."

Dolores looks from Teddy to Rashid. "A bionic leg?"

"We looked at pictures of artificial legs," says Rashid. "Paco doesn't have to be in a wheelchair. He can walk again."

"Yes. The doctors told me." Dolores smiles. "And you know what? The doctors say he is waking up."

Teddy becomes serious. "He is?"

"Yes, we can go see him. They think it will be good for him."

Rashid watches Teddy and Dolores go through the doors to the ICU. *Be brave little man*, he thinks. Rashid lived in a time of war. He remembers the injured people in Syria. They were not always happy when they woke up.

Teddy and Dolores go into a large room with a lot of beds. It is dark, but there is light from the machines next to each bed. Dolores takes Teddy's hand, and they go to Paco's bed. Paco's eyes are closed. There are burns on his face. One of his hands is covered.

"Paco?" says Dolores.

"No," says Paco. His eyes are closed.

"Honey," Dolores takes Paco's good hand.

"Go away." Paco pulls his hand back. Then he starts to move. Dolores and Teddy step back. Tears leak from Paco's closed eyes. Suddenly, he cries, "No! Go! Leave me alone!"

Dolores and Teddy do not want to upset him, so they turn and leave. Outside the ICU, Dolores is shaking. Teddy is confused. His father is awake, but he is not the same man.

Dolores comes back home to sleep, and so does Teddy. At first, he likes to be in his own bed, but his life is different. He does not do his homework. He is often late to school. His clothes are not clean. The people from church bring dinner, so there is always food. Sometimes there is dessert.

Teddy often eats dessert for breakfast. His mother does not stop him. She is not the same person, either. She does not eat much, and her eyes look red and tired. He tries making eggs for her, but they turn black in the pan. Dolores smiles at him. She takes a bite of the burned eggs. Then she throws them away.

When Dolores goes to the hospital, Teddy goes to Kyle's. "It's better that way," she explains. "Your father is not ready to see people." Then she looks scared. "He has trouble talking," she explains. "And he's very, very sad."

"What's going to happen?"

"I don't know. Your father has to make a decision."

"What kind of decision?"

"He has to decide if he *wants* to get better."

One day, Teddy comes home from school, and the yard looks different. The leaves are in bags by the street. Teddy goes inside. The house is clean. It smells like Mexican food. He can hear a woman in the kitchen say, "Teddy?"

"*Abuela*?" he says.

Teddy's grandmother comes out of the kitchen. She is a small woman with white hair. She hugs Teddy. "This house looked terrible," she says. "I spent all day cleaning."

"I didn't know you were coming," says Teddy.

"Your grandfather and I drove all night."

"From Mexico?"

"Mexico is not so far away. You need to visit us more often!"

"I guess it's because of my dad's job."

"Your dad's job?"

"He was in an accident," says Teddy.

"Yes, we know. I heard about it at my church—in Mexico! A woman there knows your mother. She asked me about Paco. I said 'He's fine, why?' and she said, 'Well, I heard he was in an accident.' And I said, 'No, that's a mistake because

Dolores would tell me.'" Abuela shakes her head. "Your mother didn't tell me!"

"I guess she wasn't thinking," says Teddy.

"No, she wasn't. Someone needs to take care of you two. Now go say 'hello' to Papa. He's in the back."

Teddy goes outside to see his grandfather.

"Hi, Papa," he says.

Papa is happy to see Teddy. He needs someone to hold the bag for the leaves. "It's a difficult time," he says while they work, "but your *abuela* will make it better."

Teddy knows that his *abuela* will not let him eat dessert for breakfast. But he is relieved she is here. He wants someone to put his family back together.

15. Home

The days get shorter and colder. Teddy and his grandfather often walk before dinner. They talk to other families on Summer Street. One night, they see Joe and his younger son Ethan. Ethan is riding on Joe's shoulders.

"My camel!" says Ethan. He pulls his father's hair and laughs.

They walk down Summer Street together. People are hanging red, green, and gold lights around their windows and on trees. Teddy holds Papa's hand and looks at Joe with Ethan. He remembers last year when Paco was home. They put gold lights around their blue and white house. This year, their house is dark.

Dolores is often in the kitchen with her mother. They cook, drink tea, and talk. Abuela slowly learns about Dolores's life with Paco and Teddy. "I love him, Mama," Dolores says. "'In sickness and in health.' That's what I said when we married, and I mean it."

"I know you do," her mother says.

"Good," says Dolores. "Because he needs all of us right now."

At dinner, Dolores tells them good news. Paco is slowly getting better. He is talking again. "And Karl says Paco was lucky. Only part of the building exploded. It could have been worse."

"What happens next?" Abuela puts food on everyone's plate.

"Karl asked Paco to stay in his job," Dolores says.

"What?" Abuela almost drops the plate.

"Karl believes in Paco now," Dolores explains. "He fired Bunny."

"Was she responsible for the accident?"

"Yes, in a way. She left the warehouse door open for the workers."

"She's sorry now!" says Abuela.

"I guess," says Dolores. "She doesn't have a job, but she's lucky. She has both her legs!"

"How does Paco feel about going back to work?"

"I don't know."

"How do you feel?" Abuela asks.

"I don't like it, but I want Paco to be happy again. Maybe he needs a purpose."

Abuela shakes her head. She is about to speak, but Papa wants to talk. "Dolores is right. Paco needs to feel useful. He wants to take care of his family."

The next day, Dolores gets a call. Paco is coming home.

Everyone works to get the house ready. Abuela and Dolores clean and cook. Teddy and Papa buy a tree and lights. They want to put lights outside, but Abuela says "no." Papa is too old, and Teddy is too small. Teddy says it is an adventure, but Abuela does not care. Rashid hears them, and he comes over. He likes to climb trees, so he hangs the lights when Abuela is not looking.

"You're brave!" says Teddy.

"Because I climb trees or because I don't listen to your grandmother?" Rashid laughs.

"Both," says Teddy.

That night, Joe goes to the hospital with Dolores. When they return, Joe takes out a wheelchair. They lift Paco into the chair. He is not heavy, but it takes time. Then Joe pushes Paco into the house and quickly says good-bye. He wants to give the family time alone.

Paco seems smaller than Teddy remembers. He still has injuries on his face, and he cannot use his hand yet. His right foot is gone. Teddy watches and waits. *I don't want this dad,* Teddy thinks. *I want my old dad.* He feels bad, and he looks down.

Paco finally starts talking. "It's good to be home," he says. He asks Papa about his garden. "Do you still have fruit trees?" he asks.

"Yes, the same ones."

Then Paco turns to Abuela. "Thank you for coming," he says. "I know it's hard to be here."

"Why do you say that?" Abuela says.

"I let you down. I promised to be a good husband and take care of Dolores."

"You are a good husband," Dolores says quietly. "Nothing has changed!"

"I'm broken," Paco says. "I'm not a good father, either." He looks at Teddy. "I'm so sorry, son."

"Stop talking like that," says Abuela. Her voice is loud, and Paco looks scared.

"Mama," says Dolores. "Be nice. Paco just got home."

"He's afraid of me," Abuela tells Dolores. "He works with dangerous chemicals. He saves people's lives, and he's afraid of a little old woman."

"You can be scary," says Dolores.

"I just want him to understand," says Abuela. She turns to Paco. "You are not alone. Don't forget that! You have a wife, a son, Papa, and me! And you also have those nice neighbors down the street."

Paco turns to Teddy. "That's your *abuela*," he says. "She won't let me feel sorry for myself."

"Right! Don't blame yourself. It was an accident. And you're not broken!" Abuela says. "Well, maybe a little."

"A little?" Paco looks at his one leg.

Teddy looks at his grandmother and then at his father. For the second time, something changes. His father might not be strong, but Teddy can be. "Abuela's right, dad," he says.

"That I'm just a little broken?"

"No, dad. You have us. We're going to help, but you need to be brave."

Paco nods. "I know, Teddy. Sometimes it's hard, though."

"Can I tell you a secret?" says Teddy.

"I'd like to hear it," says Paco.

"It gets easier."

Paco nods. "Like buying a donut."

"Exactly! So, here's the plan. First, we're going to get you a new leg. Rashid says you can walk again. Then you're going to teach me how to ride a bike."

"It's a good plan," says Paco, "but . . ."

"It's a very good plan, and we are going to do it. OK, dad?" says Teddy.

Paco looks surprised. He looks at Dolores. Then he smiles at his son. "OK, Teddy. Let's do it."